3-C

REHEMA'S JOURNEY
A VISIT IN TANZANIA
by Barbara A. Margolies

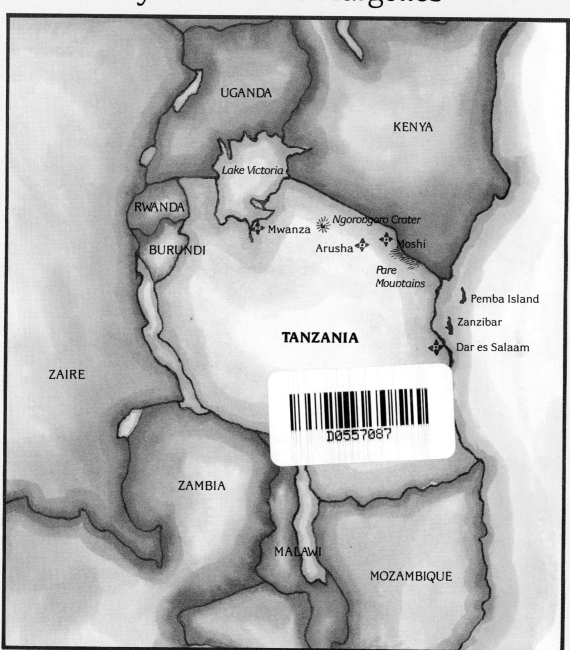

UGANDA

KENYA

Lake Victoria

RWANDA

Ngorongoro Crater

Mwanza

Arusha   Moshi

BURUNDI

Pare
Mountains

Pemba Island

Zanzibar

TANZANIA

Dar es Salaam

ZAIRE

D0557087

ZAMBIA

MALAWI

MOZAMBIQUE

SCHOLASTIC INC.

New York   Toronto   London   Auckland   Sydney

For my family, Ira, Ilisa, and Gregory,
and my dear friend Martin M. Pegler
—the winds beneath my wings.

B.A.M.

ISBN 0-590-42847-0

Copyright © 1990 by Barbara A. Margolies.
All rights reserved. Published by Scholastic Inc.

BLUE RIBBON is a registered trademark of Scholastic Inc.

12 11 10 9 8 7 6 5 4 3 2 1   6   1 2 3 4 5 6/9

Printed in the U.S.A.   08

FOREWORD

Most foreign visitors come to Tanzania just to see our fabulous wildlife in the national game parks. But few visitors take the time or have the interest to really *see* our country and meet our people, and to learn about their daily lives.

Barbara Margolies has visited Tanzania frequently and has become personally involved with many families in my country. Here, through Rehema, she hopes that children from all over the world will be able to take a glimpse of life in Tanzania.

Anthony B. Nyakyi
Ambassador
Permanent Representative
of the United Republic of Tanzania
to the United Nations

AUTHOR'S NOTE

Of all the far-away places in the world I have visited, the east African country of Tanzania is one of the most beautiful, its people among the most hospitable.

A few years ago, my long-time friend and guide, Iddi Mfangavo, honored me with an invitation to meet his family, who live in the remote and rugged Pare Mountains of northeastern Tanzania.

When I met Iddi's daughter, Rehema, I was instantly captivated by her friendly smile and her lively interest in the world beyond the mountains.

This is a story about Rehema's first trip away from home.

B.A.M.

Jambo! This is how we say hello in my country, Tanzania. My name is Rehema Mfangavo. I am nine years old. I live with my family high up in the Pare Mountains.

This is my family. The three-year-olds, Zahina and Zahara, are twins. They always dress alike. My big brother Hamisi is twelve years old and little Magid is only five. I am closest to my sister Fatuma. She's seven.

We're waiting for Baba—that's my father—to come home. I'm on vacation from school and Baba is taking only me to see the animals that live in the big game park in the Ngorongoro Crater! It will be my first trip away from home!

This is our brand new house. It is made of cement. Our old house is made of mud and cow dung. Mama still cooks there.

"Salama, Bibi." That means "Hello, Grandmother!" Bibi lives even further up the mountain. She walks down every day to help Mama. I help, too. Early in the morning I wash Zahina... but she doesn't like it very much!

We grow maize, bananas, and beans on our farm.
And every day, we gather wood for the cooking fire.

When Baba arrives Mama can start cooking. She puts bananas and beans in a large black iron pot that sits on rocks over the fire.

After lunch Mama and Hamisi wash the dishes. Before Baba
put in our new water pipe, Hamisi and I had to carry water down
the mountain—without spilling it! Now we get water right
outside our house.

Finally, my trip with Baba starts! Baba works for a travel company. He takes visitors from all over the world to the Ngorongoro Crater and also to other game parks in Tanzania. He teaches people about the wild animals and plants in the parks. Now it's my turn to visit!

We have to walk down the mountain road to get the bus that goes to Arusha town. It's the first stop on our journey. I've never been to a big city before. It's exciting but I'm a little scared, too — even though I'll be with Baba. I've never been away from Mama for a whole week!

The bus is crowded and hot. I'm lucky to have a seat next to an open window. I see a boy taking care of the family cows, and children carrying heavy loads on their heads.

Some mothers are washing clothes in a stream. There hasn't been enough rain so the water has dried up. Washing clothes in puddles is hard work! My mama is lucky to have a water pipe!

Near Tengeru, we pass a school that looks just like mine. In Tanzania, boys and girls read, write, and learn math in Swahili. We also learn how to plant and care for tea and coffee bushes, vegetables, fruit, and flowers.

Even when we're on vacation from school, we help to weed the school gardens. At harvest time, we sell what we have grown at the market. We use the money to buy chalk, pencils, and paper.

Lo-o-o! Look at all that water! Baba says it comes from a natural spring under the ground. The boy's boat is made of tree logs tied together with grass! I wish I could take a ride on it, too!

The sign says, "Welcome to Arusha town." There are so many cars and trucks! So many people! So much noise! I stay close to Baba as we walk to the New Arusha Hotel.

On my first night in Arusha the city sounds keep me awake. In my house in the mountains, I fall asleep to crickets singing and owls hooting. I miss my family!

The next morning I go
to my first church service.

There are babies being baptized; and James and
Patrick, the sons of Baba's friend, are being
confirmed at the Arusha Town Lutheran Church.

After church we go to a party at their house to celebrate.

Here are Patrick and James. That's not a book; it's really a cake! Lo-o-o! I wish I could save a piece for Fatuma. Tonight I'm going to be too full to fall asleep!

Tomorrow we leave Arusha. Finally, I will see where Baba works!

Early the next day we stop at the market to buy food for our ride to the crater. The market is colorful and *very* crowded. Look at the piles of salt!

Here is a bundle of sticks called *miswaki.* We use miswaki to clean our teeth. When I chew on the end of miswaki, it becomes a brush!

I have just enough time to buy a pineapple and some mangoes before we begin the long drive to Ngorongoro.

Just outside Arusha town we see round houses with thatched roofs. They are very different from my house. People of the Waarusha tribe live in the round houses. The Waarusha girl has the same chores as me—I have to gather firewood, too!

Lo-o-o! The Waarusha boy has painted his face white! Baba tells me that it's part of a ceremony boys go through to become men. The boy wears a blade of grass on his forehead so that he will have a good life.

Tumefika! Hooray! We're at the crater!

As we drive down to the crater floor, Baba tells me about the animals and how people all over the world are helping to save them. It's exciting to be so close to the wild animals. But it's also scary, and it can be dangerous, too. Baba says you must always stay inside the car and *never* put your hands outside the window!

We see lions, an ostrich,

zebras,

an elephant,

wildebeest,

hippopotamuses,

cheetahs,

and a black rhinoceros.

It makes me very sad when Baba tells me there are so few rhinoceroses left in Africa. Poachers hunt and kill them for their horns, even though it's against the law. When park rangers find poachers, they put them in jail.

Too soon, it's time to say *kwaheri* to all the beautiful animals. One day I will come back to visit them again.

Just outside the crater we pass a Maasai village. Baba sees his Maasai friends, Ngaapa Ndoroko and Malunga Nangary. They are *morans*, or warriors.

The red cloth they wear is called *olubega* in Maasai language. The warriors always carry *olalem*, long knives.

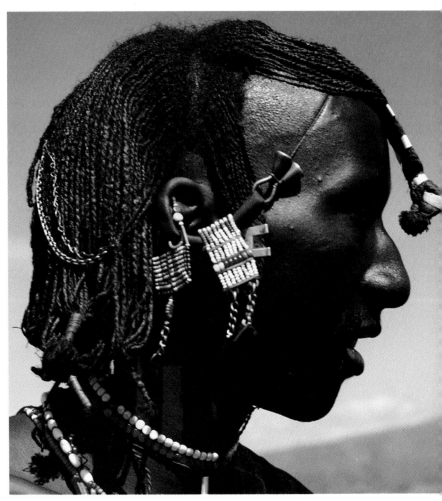

The morans rub red ochre, a mineral from the earth mixed with animal fat, into their long hair. The morans seem to wear as much jewelry as the women!

Baba knows all about the Maasai people. They are different from other tribes. They do not have farms to grow food. Instead, they own cows and goats. The Maasai are nomads because when their cattle have eaten all the grass in one place, they move to another place where their animals can find new grass. The milk and blood of the cows are very important foods to the Maasai.

The Maasai house is different from the Waarusha house and from my house in the mountains. The Maasai house is made of sticks and grass and covered with cow dung. Lo-o-o! I miss my own house. When I hear Baba say *ole sere*, good-bye in Maasai, I know we're going home.

The ride back to the Pare Mountains seems to go quickly. When the road gets very, very bumpy, it means my house is near.

That night as the sun sets, I think about all the wonderful people I've met, all the beautiful animals I've seen. School starts tomorrow and Baba must go back to his job in Arusha town. I won't see him again until the rainy season in May. I will miss Baba! But I will always remember the special journey we took together.

Kwaheri. Good-bye.

Some Swahili Words from Rehema's Journey

Word	Translation	Pronunciation
Arusha	(name of a city)	(a * ROO * sha)
Bibi	(grandmother)	(BI * bi)
Jambo	(hello)	(JA * mbow)
Kwaheri	(good-bye)	(kwa * HE * ri)
Maasai	(name of a tribe)	(MA * sai)
Miswaki	(a "toothbrush")	(mi * SWA * ki)
Ngorongoro	(name of a crater)	(nn * go * row * NGO * row)
Pare	(name of mountain range)	(PA * re)
Rehema Mfangavo		(re * HE * mah) (mmfah * NGA * vo)
Salama	(a greeting)	(sa * LA * ma)
Tanzania	(name of a country)	(tan * zah * KNEE * ah)
Tumefika	(Hooray, we've arrived!)	(toome * FI * kah)
Tengeru	(name of a village)	(te * NGE * roo)
Waarusha	(name of a tribe)	(wah * ROO * sha)

How do you say "cake" in Swahili? Here are some words you can learn to say in Swahili.

cake	(keki)	(KE * ki)
chalk	(chaki)	(CHA * ki)
cheetah	(duma)	(DOO * ma)
elephant	(tembo)	(TEM * bow)
farm	(shamba)	(SHAM * bah)
hippopotamus	(kiboko)	(ki * BOW * kow)
lion	(simba)	(SIM * bah)
lunch	(chakula cha mchana)	(cha * KOO * la) (CHA) (mm * CHA * nah)
ostrich	(mbuni)	(mm * BOO * ni)
paper	(karatasi)	(kah * rah * TAH * si)
pencil	(penseli)	(pen * SE * li)
rhinoceros	(kifaru)	(ki * FAH * roo)
wildebeest	(nyumbu)	(n * YOOM * boo)
school	(shule)	(SHOO * le)
zebra	(punda milia)	(POON * dah) (mi * LIAH)